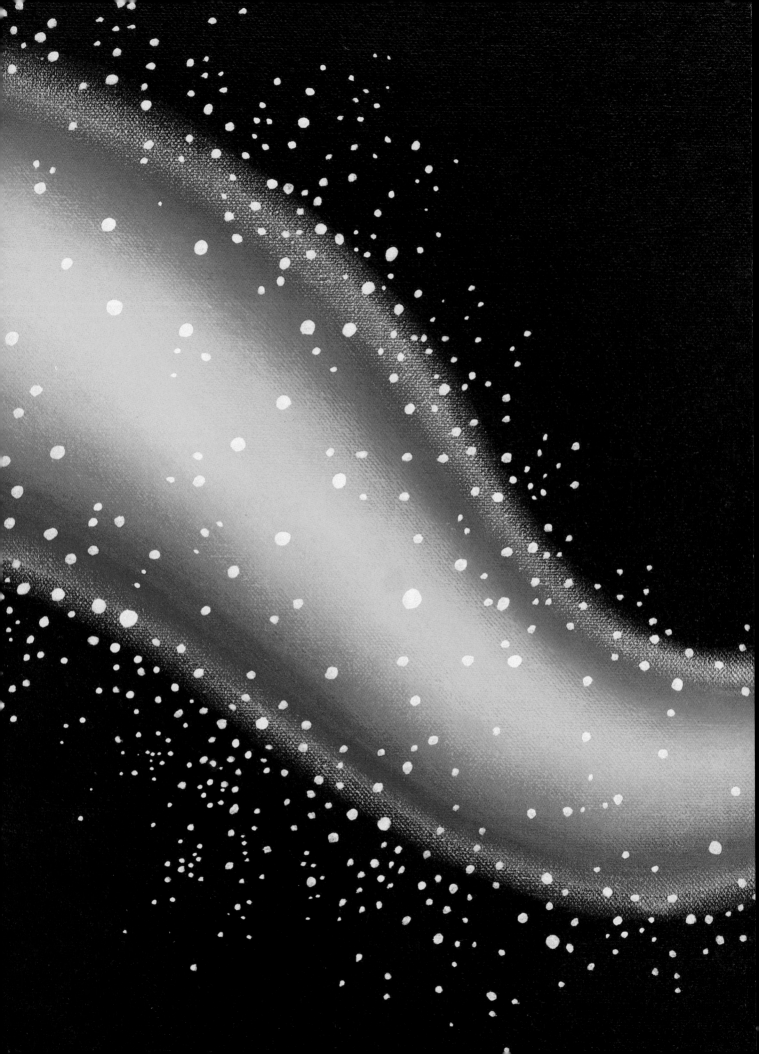

THE DREAM STEALER

by

Stephen E. Cosgrove

illustrated by

Carol Heyer

Graphic Arts Center Publishing Company
Portland, Oregon

International Standard Book Number 1-55868-009-8
Library of Congress Number 89-83843
Text © MCMLXXXIX by Stephen E. Cosgrove
Illustrations © MCMLXXXIX by Carol Heyer
All rights reserved. No part of this book
can be reproduced by any means
without written permission of the publisher.
Published by Graphic Arts Center Publishing Company
P.O. Box 10306 • Portland, Oregon 97210 • 503/226-2402
Editor-in-Chief • Douglas A. Pfeiffer
Associate Editor • Jean Andrews
Designer • Becky Gyes
Typographer • Harrison Typesetting, Inc.
Color House • Spectrum West
Printer • Dynagraphics, Inc.
Bindery • Lincoln & Allen
Printed in the United States of America

To Richard Burhans.
For if you truly believe,
dreams all can and do come true.
STEPHEN

Beyond where the sun does set, farther than the rainbow falls, on an island in the middle of a swamp, a strange hunch-backed gnome silently sat on a gaily bridled goat watching daylight turn to dusk, turn to dark. Strapped to his goat were two leather bags—one full, one empty.

Silent, still, he sat until the night was at its darkest. Then, and only then, he broke the eerie silence and laughed at the moon rising full. He spun his goat in circles and chanted loudly,

> *"My bag is filled with nightmares, it seems,*
> *Which I will trade for your sweet dreams.*
> *The dreams are mine; the nightmares yours,*
> *But soon there will be dreams no more.*
> *The bells will peal, and as they ring,*
> *I, the Dream Stealer, shall be king!"*

Then, in a puff of twisted mist and darkened cloud, he disappeared into the forest.

ot far from
the swamp, wrapped in the silvered shadows of the autumn
moon, was the village of Chimera.
Cottages—with their patched,
thatched roofs and chimneys
made from river rock—lined the
cobbled streets that twisted and
twirled like taffy throughout the
village.

This was the town where lived
brother and sister, Gabby and
Michael McDool. Gabby was eight
and loved to talk as much as she
loved to dream. She talked to
anyone who would listen and to
many who wouldn't. Michael was
thirteen, a strapping youth who
worked for his father as a smithy's
apprentice.

In early evening's light, mother
McDool would light a candle and
leave it in the open attic window. In
this way, Michael and Gabby knew
that supper was nearly cooked and
that tools should be put away. The
workday was done.

Down long, twisted lanes at the outside edge of Chimera stood a quaint old home built of seasoned polepine and quarried rock. It was here that a charming old hermit lived and had lived forever and a day. He had silvered hair, a long flowing beard to match, and eyes that sparkled crystal blue. His hair swirled about him on windy days, as his gnarled feet, set in soft-sewn boots, glided over the cobbled streets.

His name was Bartholomew and he was the town's librarian, the keeper—the custodian if you like—of all of Chimera's fine, leather-bound books. Wherever he walked, wherever he went, Bartholomew carried books—no matter the title, no matter the stories. Books, all marvelous stories filled with wishes and wants.

Of all the books he tended, he would lend them to children and parents alike. He would take books to the old and infirm so that their minds might journey to places their feet couldn't take them. As he had often said to any who would listen, "For inside books are delicious, magical places that will stir the imagination of any who wish to read the words written inside."

Now, here in shadowed moonlight, Bartholomew's step quickened. He was eager for a warm fire and a hot tidy bowl of stew. For it was eventide in Chimera.

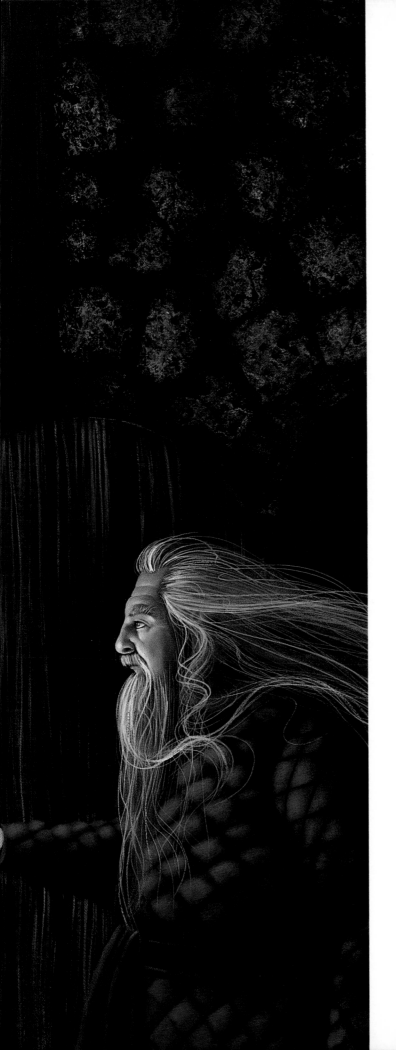

But all was not sweetness and light in Chimera. For nearly every night, when the time was seven minutes past the ringing of the eleventh hour, children throughout the village woke crying in their sleep from dreams gone bad.

Wooden matches sputtered and flared to life, lighting waxy candles' wicks, as warm feet plopped onto cold tile. Flickering lights floated from window to window, as parents quickly padded down paneled hallways to soothe away the fears of their children.

One brightly moonlit night, Bartholomew watched and listened to all these goings-on from his shuttered windows that were opened wide. Robed and in slippered feet, he slipped out into the night to see what he might see.

The old storyteller watched in wide-eyed wonder as a shadowy shape scurried from cottage to cottage. This phantom had two leather bags draped over his shoulders—one full, one empty.

Bartholomew watched the shape slip up and over the wooden sill of an unshuttered window, and into one of the Chimeran homes. As the old man peeked through the window, the shadowed shape, walking crablike, stole up to a sleeping child bundled on her sleeping pallet. The form reached into one of his bags, taking from it a squirming bit of blackened cloud.

The cloud was cast like a net over the bed and the twisting form danced upon the night. Slowly it dropped, wrapping the child in its dark and dreary form. When the cloud surrounded the child, out popped a bright and glittering rainbow that was soon grabbed and stuffed into the empty bag.

The child tossed and whimpered in her sleep; another dream gone bad. Out the way he had come, the thief slipped back into the night.

The creature of night and fright repeated his exercise until one bag was empty and the other was filled. His mission completed, the shadowy shape stepped full into the moon's soft-focused glow. The shadows paled, and there in that light, Bartholomew spied the Dream Stealer with the squiggling bag of rainbow dreams tossed over his shoulder. With a twisted smile, he leapt to the back of his rearing goat and trotted silently away.

"Oh, dear me," Bartholomew gasped, "it is he who causes the children to cry out!"

He rushed back to his cottage, worried and concerned. There he muttered and fussed, as he poured hot tea into a china cup.

"Tomorrow," said he, "I must follow this stealer of dreams. If I don't, all the dreams of the children will be gone. Without dreams, the village of Chimera is doomed."

With teacup and saucer rattling in hand, he went to his library stacked with books. There he sat and read throughout the night, filling his mind with sparkling plans and imagination. He would need all this and more to recapture the lost dreams of the children.

Early the next morning as the sun stretched golden ribbons from tree to tree, Bartholomew woke with a start. He quickly dressed and rushed into the cobbled street in search of Michael McDool, a necessary partner in his plan.

He found Michael already hard at work hammering at his anvil in the smithy shop. Quietly he told the boy of his plan to follow the creature and recover the lost dreams.

"And so, Michael," he said, "I'll be needing your help. Between the two of us it can be done. For I am not strong enough to capture this gnome alone and release the dreams at the same time."

Michael hurriedly banked the forge and they would have been on their way—save for Michael's little sister, Gabby. Down she hopped from the loft above babbling away, "Oh, please, can I go, too? Please! Please! Please! For the dreams that were stolen were partly mine. Oh, I must go. I must!"

They reluctantly agreed, or rather had to agree, for she would tag along no matter what—the what being she would probably get lost along the way.

Together, this tiny band of three rushed to seek the permission of Michael and Gabby's parents. Now the McDools were simple folk, but most of all, they were grown-up and really didn't believe in dreams. They laughed politely at the old man's story. Since all the chores were done, they casually gave their permission. For Bartholomew had often taken the children of Chimera on walks and talks in the forest, and this surely was just a lark.

Gabby's mother made them a lunch of plump sausage and fluffy biscuits, and wrapped it all tight in a checkered cloth. Then, hand-in-hand, Bartholomew, Michael, and Gabby walked out of the village in the direction taken by the thief of dreams the night before.

Once outside the village, upon close investigation they found and followed the cloven-hoofed tracks of the Dream Stealer's goat. On and on they marched, beyond the meadow and alongside Reverie River, which gently flowed through the land.

After what seemed like hours and hours, they came to the rapids, where the river was joined by the Stream of Dreams. Here the water rushed, rolled, and roared over boulders and rocks. The quest nearly ended, for Gabby was frightened by all the noise, and unfortunately, the tracks definitely led across the rushing water.

They couldn't just leave her there, though it was a strong temptation. Finally, Michael lifted her upon his broad back and forded the waters. Bartholomew, with his robes wrapped 'round his waist and humming a brave little tune, stepped from stone to stone and followed.

Once safely on the other side, their search continued, as the sun dried sandals, boots, and trousers. Step by step, they carefully followed the mud-set tracks of the heavily-laden goat.

The trail wandered alongside the river and disappeared into a group of trees. Now these were not ordinary trees, but rather a tangled jangle of limbs and leaves called Phantom Forest. Here, the mists twisted and snaked about the trunks and bushes, scaring any who dared to enter.

Oh, and yes, the forest was frightening. Ghosts and goblins slipped and swirled about their legs and twisted into their minds, as they inched along the path. Fear, like fingernails raked down a blackboard, caused the hair on the back of their necks to creep and their eyes to open wide.

Look, there! Was that a witch behind that tree? And there! Was that a hobgoblin or a ghoul sneaking in the shadows ready to leap?

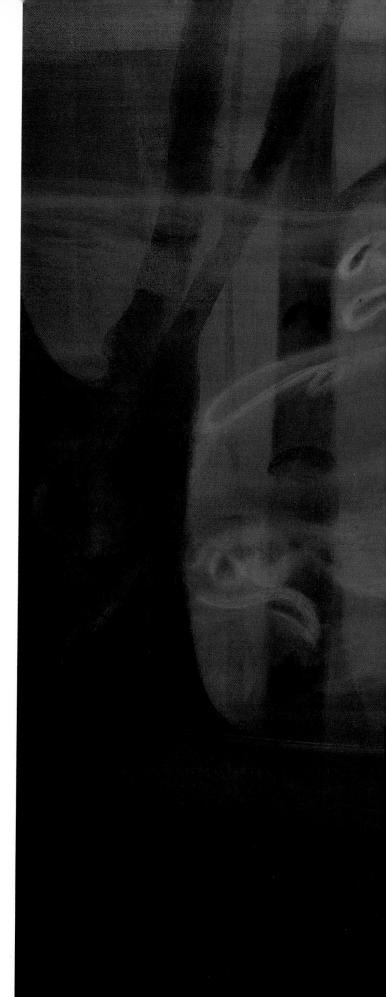

Their heads snapped to and fro, and they would have been conquered, vanquished by their imaginations, if Bartholomew had not come to his senses. "This is silly," said he with more gusto than he felt. "This is nothing more than mist. How can we win over the Dream Stealer if we can't win over our own fears?"

With that, they sat upon the green-moss grasses and bravely spread their picnic out on the checkered cloth. Filled with a false bravado, they munched their lunch and softly first, then louder later, began to laugh at all their minds had made. Little by little, the mists lifted and the fearsome became frivolous, as the witches turned into white-bark trees, and the hobgoblins changed back to lilac bushes.

As they sat, picking at the crumbs of fluffy biscuits and licking the tangy taste of sausage from their fingers, they heard odd music lilting from deep in the forest. Quickly scampering ahead to a tiny rise, below they spied the most peculiar sight. There, surrounded by a moat of swamp, was a mist-shrouded island.

Near the center of the island was a cave guarded by vine-draped bars. In a clearing, near the cave, was a smouldering cookfire. Hanging over the fire on a twisted stick was a cauldron that bubbled and burped. From the pot leaked and limped shadowy shapes, darkened clouds of twisted imagination. Behind the cauldron, standing near the fire, was the hunch-backed gnome himself, singing as he tossed odd bits of this and that into the glop.

While they watched secretly, the Dream Stealer danced about in a whirling dervish, singing this frenzied song.

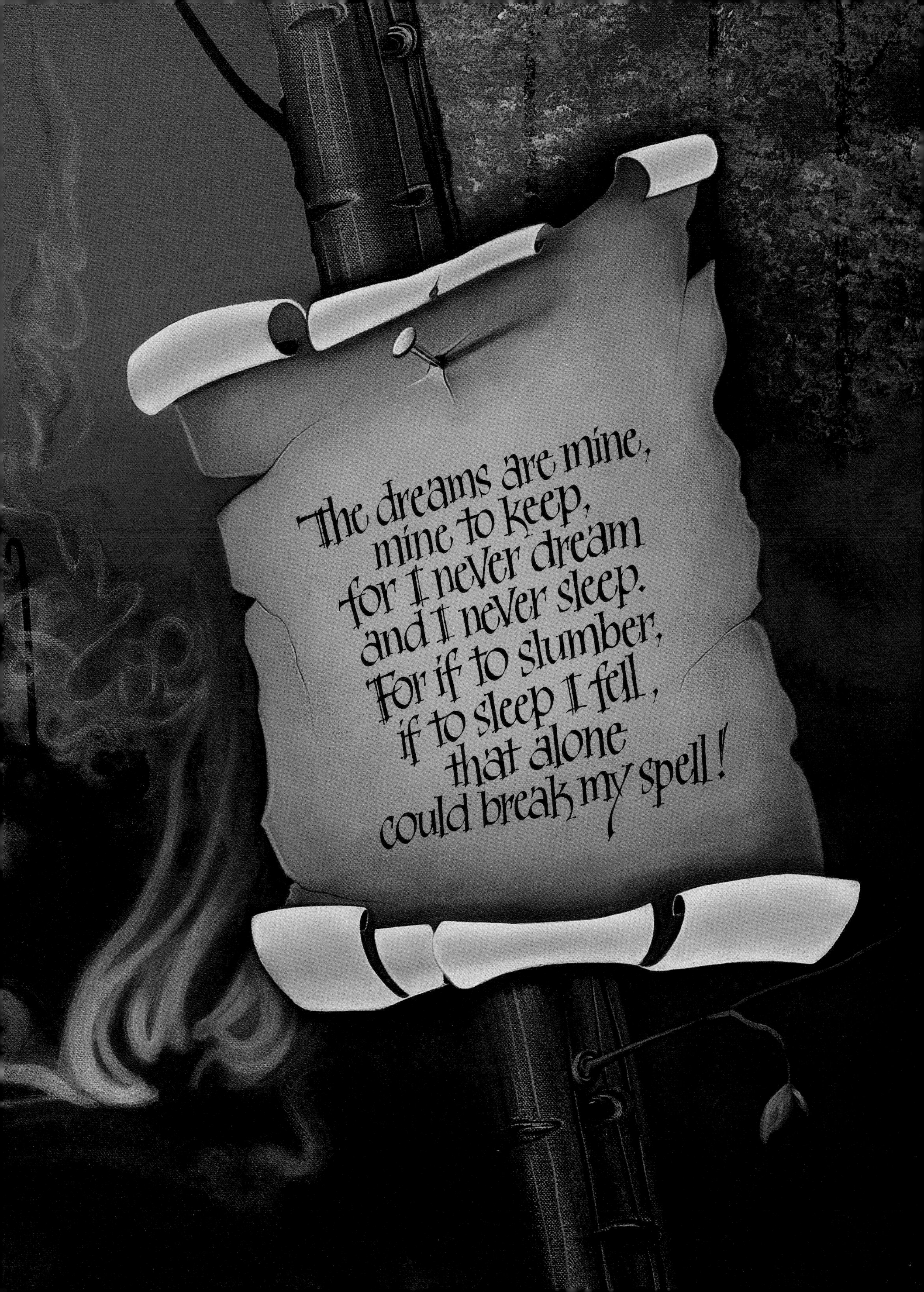

The dreams are mine,
   mine to keep,
   for I never dream
   and I never sleep.
   For if to slumber,
   if to sleep I fell,
   that alone
   could break my spell!

"That's the answer," whispered Michael, "simply put the Dream Stealer to sleep."

"Oh, pooh," snipped Gabby, "we can't just walk down into his swamp and say, 'Here's your pillow and blanket, Mr. Dream Stealer, sir. It's time to go nonny-nonny.'"

"Shh!" hushed Bartholomew, "We'll stick to my original plan and allow ourselves to somehow get captured. Once in the camp, Michael will grab the gnome and I will free the dreams."

Gabby looked at Bartholomew like he had just gone mad. "And how do you suppose we can 'somehow' get captured?"

"Maybe by me and my chums!" a cackling voice cracked.

They snapped their heads around at the sound. There, at their feet, stood the hunch-backed gnome himself, and a small army of wispy nightmare forms. Surrounded by their own fears, they were captured and quickly led down to the island camp.

The Dream Stealer paced about and laughed in glee. "You three are just what I need," he gloated. "I'll charm you and bewitch you like my old goat over there. Then, I'll be able to carry even more dreams from Chimera. When all the dreams are gone, the land shall be mine and I shall be king of a delightfully dreary place."

As the would-be king railed about the boiling pot, Bartholomew winked at Michael, who stood slowly as the gnome turned his back. With outstretched hands, he started towards the gnome and would have caught him then and there, except Gabby, who just didn't know when to be quiet, blurted out loudly, "Be careful, Michael! Don't trip on that root!"

Michael turned at the sound of his sister's voice and, sure enough, tripped on the root. He bumped his head on a rock and lay there, silent-still, knocked unconscious.

"Oh, no!" cried Gabby, as Bartholomew looked on in shock, his well-laid plans gone astray.

A tear dripped from her eye as Gabby realized what she had done, but, of course, the more excited or frightened she became, the more she talked. The more she talked, the more she thought to talk about. Gabby wasn't excited now, but she was frightened near to distraction.

"Oh, dear me," she babbled, "this reminds me of the time that my mother and my father were afeared of an old bear that wandered in from the woods. Oh, they were scared and I was scared and we were all scared together. We waited until the hunter came and he . . ." She rattled on and on talking of this and that.

Bored to exhaustion by the never-ending story, the Dream Stealer's attention wandered. Soon, his eyelids grew so heavy that he fell fast asleep. As his snarkled snores echoed through the swamp, all of his created nightmares froze in place—riveted by Gabby's gabbing.

Michael raised up from the dust, shook his head and dazedly asked, "What happened?"

"Shh, follow me," whispered Bartholomew. "Gabby, don't stop talking, no matter what happens."

Michael ripped open the vine-like bars and the two slipped into the cave, as Gabby babbled to the blissfully snoring gnome. Inside, the young smithy and the old librarian released the imprisoned dreams. With a *whoosh,* the dreams swirled out of the cave and into the sky, forming a rainbow of light and bright.

In a hush, the dreams rushed back to their rightful owners. As they fled, a delightful rain began to fall and Phantom Forest was filled with laughing crystal light. When this light touched the nightmare forms, all returned to what they were before—bits of imagination.

With all the dreams of the children of Chimera set free, the two started to leave the cave, but from deep inside, Michael heard a muffled sound. He turned and spied a tiny dream, trapped and crying.

"Now, now little dream, don't cry," said the young smithy, lifting the rock to free the tiny apparition. "Return to the child who owns you in Chimera."

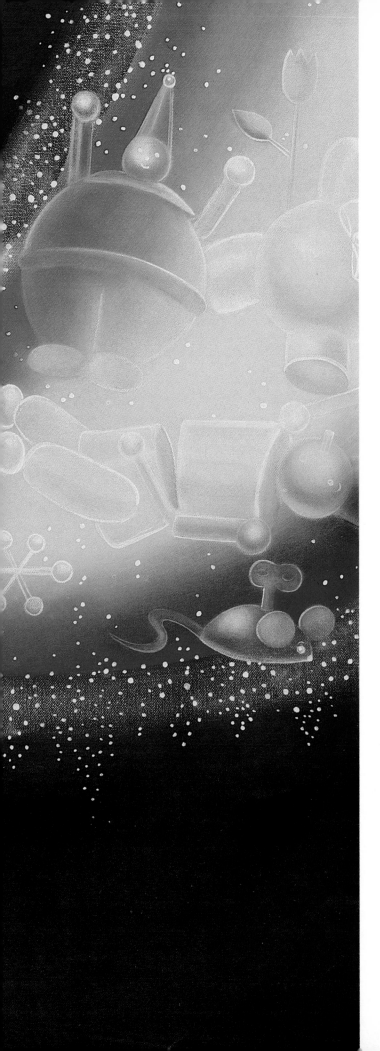

The littlest dream swirled up into the sky, but instead of rushing back to the village, it twisted around and around in sparkles of green and gold. Then, satisfied of its rightful owner, it settled happily, like a warm woolen blanket, about the shoulders of the Dream Stealer himself.

Gabby was so shocked that she stopped talking, and the forest echoed with silence as the Dream Stealer woke. She tried to resume her story and put him back to sleep, but it was too late . . . the gnome was fully awake.

But instead of being frightful and mean, the gnome yawned and stretched his arms up to the sky. "Oh, what a sleep and, oh, what wicked nightmares I had." He looked about and, with eyes growing wide, noticed Gabby, Michael, and Bartholomew. Blinking his great eyes once or twice in disbelief, he asked, "Who are you? Are you part of my dream? Am I still asleep?"

"No, you are not asleep," said Bartholomew. "But somewhere, somehow, you lost your dream and instead stole the dreams of others." Sadly then, Gabby told the gnome of the evil deeds he had done in his dreamless sleep.

"I will repay ten times over that which I have stolen," said the saddened gnome, as tears traced down his cheeks.

Then the four—Bartholomew, Michael and Gabby McDool, and the saddened but enlightened gnome—made their way back to Chimera, where lives are still based on dreams.

It matters not whether you believe this woven tale, for outside your window, even now, a gentle gnome watches over you as you slumber. He sleeps all day and watches all night, lest your sleep be broken by yet another who might come this way. Another thief of hope and dreams . . . a dream stealer.

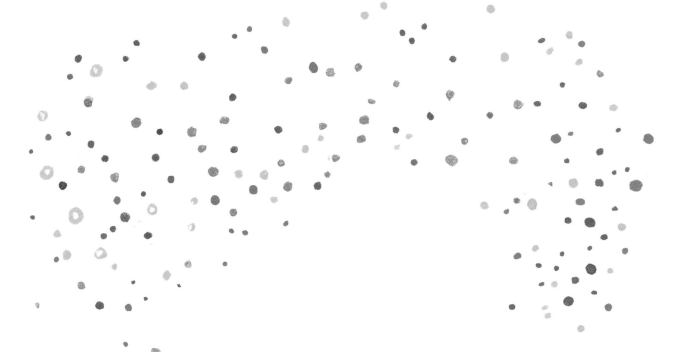

Other books in the DreamMaker Classic series:

PRANCER